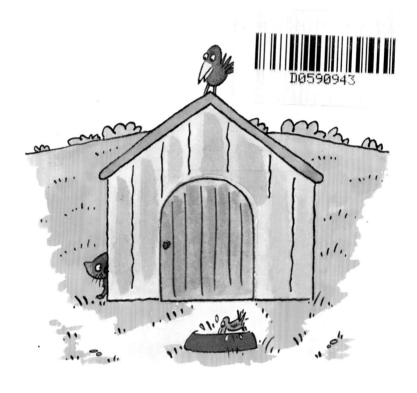

Who lives in the kennel?

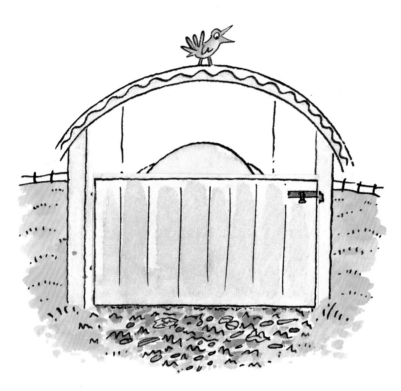

Who lives in the sty?

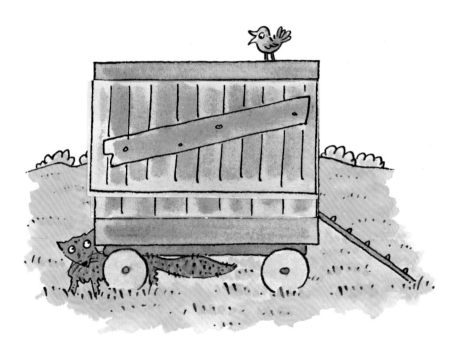

Who lives in the coop?

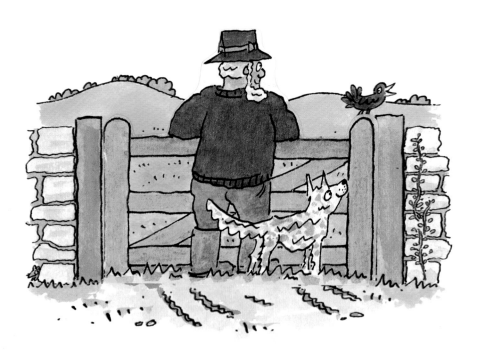

Who lives in the field?

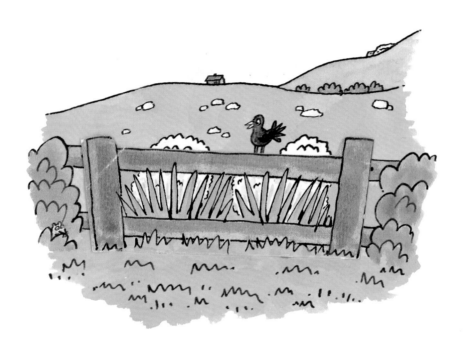

Who lives on the hills?

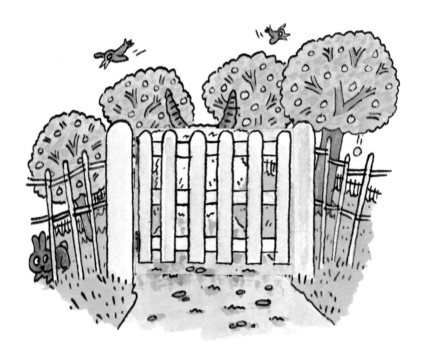

Who lives in the orchard?

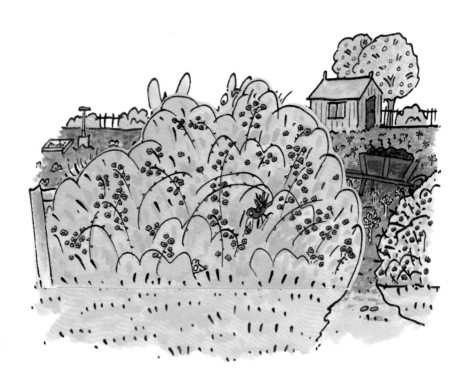

Who is in the kitchen garden?

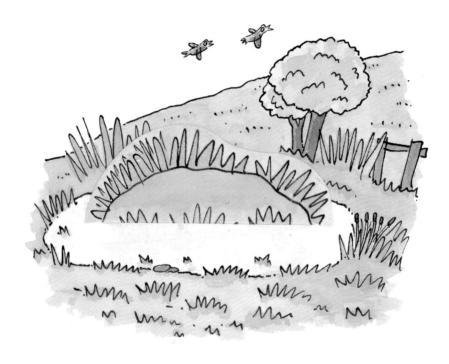

Who lives on the pond?

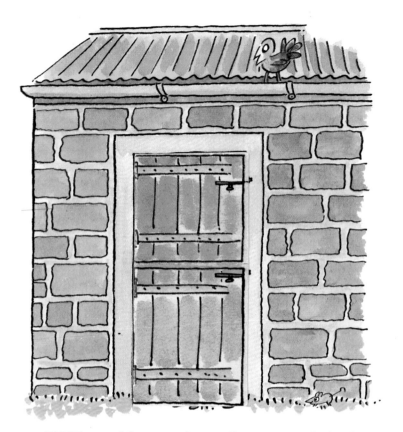

Who lives in the stable?

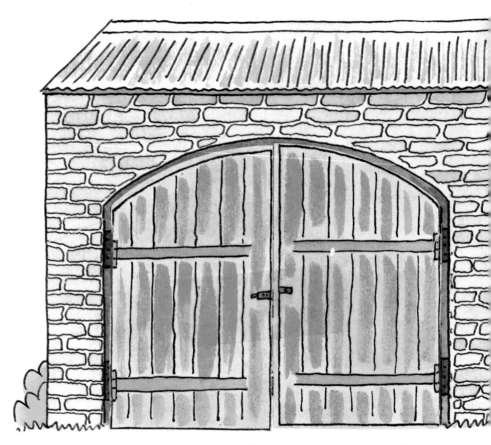

And who is in the barn?